The Dying Wish

Courttia Newland is the author of the critically acclaimed novels *The Scholar*, *Society Within* and *Snakeskin*. He has contributed to the anthologies *Disco 2000*, *New Writers 8* and *AfroBeat*, and is editor of an anthology of new black writing in Britain, *IC3*. He lives in west London.

The Dying Wish

Courttia Newland

ABACUS

First published in Great Britain in May 2006 by Abacus

A CIP catalogue record for this book
is available from the British Library.

ISBN 0 349 11963 5

Typeset by SX Composing DTP, Rayleigh, Essex

Printed and bound in Great Britain

Abacus
An imprint of
Time Warner Book Group UK
Brettenham House
Lancaster Place
London WC2E 7EN

www.twbg.co.uk

For Sharmila

ONE

Seconds after the shrill bell rang children began to emerge from the small, red-brick building. They poured from swing doors into the bright sun of the summer day, joyful smiles on many faces, eyes bright and alive with excitement. Running full pelt into the legs of the waiting adults, most, if not all, dragged colourful bags behind them, proud like hunters bringing home fresh meat. It was heart-warming just to be near that churning ocean of welcome and reunion.

I watched as kids were lifted to adult height, pressed against warm lips, spun around on the spot, knelt before and re-dressed critically yet with obvious love from parents and guardians alike. It was like a small slice of Christmas, bite-sized and easy to swallow. I was unable to stop myself smiling at the giggles and laughter.

Scanning the crowd, I saw her sprint as fast as her little legs could carry her, out of the school doors, along a path and past her friends, crashing into my own legs. She enfolded both in a tight bear hug. I bent, wincing at the twinge of discomfort that shot through my ageing bones, hugging her tiny form. It was the same every time I came to pick Akira up. I wouldn't have changed it for the world.

'Hi, Uncle Vinnie,' she said, her voice muffled by the cloth of my jeans.

'Hey you, have a good day?'

'Yeah . . .'

'Yes, not yeah . . .'

'Yes . . .'

Her forehead bashed against my legs as she nodded like a woodpecker. I grabbed Akira's hand and led her away from the school towards my battered car. It was a brown and tiny seventies-style Audi, looking slightly pitiful against all the shiny silver hatchbacks, huge people carriers and Jeeps. I'd been planning to get rid of it for over a year. I even knew the cost of a replacement, yet although I could afford it, nostalgia wouldn't let me trade the car in. Somewhere in the back of my mind I already knew I would be driving the Audi until it fell apart around me like a metal house of cards.

'What did you do in school today?'

'We had to draw trees.'

'Did you? At least you got to go out in the sunshine. It was lovely today. Is that your drawing?'

I pointed at the orange paper she was clutching in one hand. Akira nodded again.

'Can I see?'

She made a shy face, then handed it over with all the calm of a professional artist. Her mother would have been proud. I studied the drawing.

'That's very good, Akira . . . What kind of tree is that?'

'A silver birch.'

'That's very clever of you. How do you know that?'

'It says so in the corner.'

'So it does.' Sometimes she was so much like an adult, I had to look twice just to make sure I hadn't missed anything. I gave the picture back. 'Just think, pretty soon I won't be coming to pick you up from school any more. You'll be in secondary school, walking home by yourself.'

'Yeah!'

'Yes, Akira, not yeah . . .'

'Yes!'

3

She was beaming at the thought. Already, at only nine years old, freedom was a wonderful concept. I guided her to my car and opened up, smiling in pride as she scrambled into the front seat. It was something Carmen would never have allowed, yet another habit her dimples and shy smile had forced me to indulge. She sat there kicking her legs.

'All right Mrs, let's go and see your mum, okay?'

'Yeah!' Akira yelled at the top of her voice. I opened my mouth, thought about it, then started the car and we were off.

I had been employing Akira's mother for the last year or so. My business, formerly known as James' Private Investigations, had been dealing with so many new clients and high-class recommendations provided by Carmen Sinclair, the name had actually been changed six weeks before I officially took her on. Now it was called James and Sinclair's Private Investigations. My new business partner had been very pleased, although she'd thought for weeks about whether she should use her family name or the surname she'd given her daughter, which belonged to Akira's long absent father. After much agonising she decided to keep her own.

All that was left to do after that was order a set of new business cards, make a quick phone call to Yellow Pages and Thompson's local directory, then organise a sign change on my office door. I'd been against the idea of a partner for so many years I'd expected to feel anger, or maybe have a general feeling of upset when the final letter of her name was added to mine.

Happily though, I felt good. I remember hugging Carmen and Sadie, my loyal receptionist, enjoying the moment and the feeling that we were on the rise now. 'Small moves, big t'ings,' as Carmen was fond of saying. To be honest, I felt calmer than I had for a long time, less like a loner and more like the person I'd always really wanted to be: a family man.

Carmen deserved it. Not only had she assisted in the biggest case of my life, the Walker case, she'd also drummed up a huge amount of her own work. She had a separate little office that had once been my darkroom, her own computer, files and clients, as well as a growing reputation among her mostly working-class customers for being exceptional at her job. There was no doubt about it: making Carmen Sinclair my full partner was the smartest move I'd made in a while.

Akira and I reached my office block, in Farringdon, north London, which was just under an hour's drive from Peckham. I took Akira up through the corridors towards my office, though to be truthful she led for most of the way, owing to her boundless energy. When we got to my floor, she ran along the passage like a speeding underground train, straight into the legs of a woman carrying a cardboard box. The woman shrieked. The box fell out of her hands and a number of files spilled on to the dusty passage floor. Akira stood back. Even though I couldn't see her face, I instantly recognised the pose and could imagine the 'nothing-to-do-with-me' look of almost-sorrow all kids adopt when they've been caught doing wrong. I hurried my pace and began to help the woman with her files.

'I'm really sorry, she wasn't looking where she was going. Say sorry to the lady, Akira . . .'

'Sorry . . .' Her tone was mournful, filled with the expectation of trouble.

6

The woman looked up and smiled. She was East Asian, unusually pretty. One of her eyes was grey while the other was brown and her hair was so dark it captured even the poor light coming from the tubes in the ceiling. It hung in one long braid that curled down her back like a lizard before resting against her thigh. She wore a beige skirt that ended just above the knee, clear brown stockings and a cream blouse that was opened quite low. For a moment all Akira and I could do was stare.

'It's okay, no harm done . . .' Her smile grew wider. 'You're a gorgeous little girl, aren't you?' Akira looked at the floor again. Everyone knew she was acting this time. 'What's your name?' the woman continued.

'Akira,' the little girl told her. 'What's yours?'

'Lizzie,' the beautiful woman said. 'Short for Elizabeth.'

I was a little thrown by that. She didn't seem like an Elizabeth or Lizzie, and not just because she was Asian either. For some reason the name just didn't suit her. A little bell of 'not-quite-right' rang inside me. I let it go at the time, probably because I fancied her so much.

7

'You're pretty too,' Akira was saying, while I gave Lizzie the last of her files.

'Thank you,' she said, half to me and half to the little girl. She seemed eager to get away now that the chit-chat was over. I wasn't in such a hurry.

'I'm Ervine,' I told her, offering my hand. 'Ervine James. I have the office next door to yours.'

'Hello, Mr James . . .' She shook my hand loosely, as if it were a feather. Her fingers were slim, the skin smooth and soft as the surface of a balloon. She let go fast and picked up the box.

'Moving in?' I enquired, hoping she'd join the conversation. She smiled again, although it wasn't as real as the first. There were no teeth on show now. It was all cheeks and lips.

'Yes . . . I'm sorry, Mr James, but I must get on. We've got so much to do. Have a good day.'

'Call me Ervine—' I started.

I was talking to her back. The office door had closed before I was even finished. I looked at Akira, who was waiting to see what would happen next.

'C'mon darling, let's go.'

I entered my own office, a frown etched into my forehead.

Sadie was busy talking to somebody on the phone, and there was a man sitting on one of the chairs meant for clients. He was middle-aged and looked more African than West Indian I guessed. His long face was shiny and dark like a newly polished boot. His skin was so thin that it seemed to hug his cheeks, which made him look as stern as a soldier on parade. The bones of his knees stuck out beneath charcoal-grey slacks and there wasn't an ounce of fat on his entire body. I nodded his way as I entered the office. He nodded back, his deep eyes red and far away. I would have said something to him, a hello or how are you doing, but he wasn't one of mine and I didn't know why he was there. Sadie motioned at some letters while she talked. I picked them up, and then pushed through the doors into the private section of the office.

In the early days, before I took on the Walker case, my office space had been very different. The small room had been stocked with as many items from the world of TV detective movies as I could find: a coat and hat stand, a broad wooden desk, one filing cabinet that held nothing but notepads and pens, white plastic blinds on the windows.

I'd never quite realised how much damage my image was doing to business. My existing client base and most new customers I saw back then had thought I was a hack, a half-timer with one foot in the past and a head in the clouds, with no real expertise or experience to speak of. It had helped that my prices were so low they plugged me into the working-class community who couldn't afford the private investigators from Yellow Pages and the like. It also meant that I wasn't making any real money. I was suffering, both financially and emotionally. By the time Robert Walker MP came along I was on the verge of giving the whole thing up.

Walker hired me to find and bring to justice the man who'd murdered his daughter. Viali had been a bright law student, stunningly attractive, with a personality that drew people in like bees to bright flowers. She'd been killed on the South Bank believing she'd been waiting for her father, who'd had no idea such an appointment had ever been made. I took on the case, and inherited Walker's sense of shock and outrage. The more I'd found out about Viali Walker, the more mysterious the facts behind her death became. Yet by then, I'd become so attached to her memory, what she stood for and what that meant to me, that the case pretty soon became more than just a job. It grew into an obsession.

Many things changed in those months. Robert Walker died by another man's hand. I reconnected with my old friend Carmen Sinclair, along with the new addition to her life, her daughter Akira. In a sense, I suppose, a part of me died too in that brief space in time, or even became reborn as a new Ervine James. By finding Viali's killer, the experience I had been lacking had been won. What I did with that new expertise was up to me.

I got rid of the filing cabinet and white plastic blinds, and tried to make the office more homely. In fact the only thing I kept from those days was my black leather chair and the wooden desk that stood before it. I put pictures of people I admired up on the walls – Miles Davis, Muhammad Ali, Alex Haley – as well as prints of abstract paintings. I bought a new computer, a leather sofa and some smaller, comfier chairs so that clients could feel more at ease. I left the windows curtainless so that London daylight flooded the room and made it bright and welcoming rather than dark and dingy.

Lately I always managed to walk into my office and become inspired by the changes I'd made. I'd stop and look around, take a deep breath and wallow in my own sense of success. Unaware of this, Akira walked through the room without a single glance, on a mission that would not be stalled or halted for anyone or anything, least of all some middle-aged man's foolish pride. Going through another door at the opposite end of the room, she disappeared. There was an abrupt cry of a female voice, then the sound of a ton of kisses, along with squeals of delight from the little girl. I smiled at the sound and walked across to the doorway, poking my head around the frame. Akira was sitting on her mother's lap, arms wrapped tight around her.

'Afternoon,' I said.

'Afternoon.'

Carmen was still hugging her daughter,

planting kisses on her forehead and squeezing the life out of her, with one eye on the computer screen. She was a short, robust woman with bright eyes, a scattering of freckles across her pine-brown face, a laugh like a braying donkey and the attitude of ten men three times her size. We'd grown up together on the mean streets of the Claybridge Estate in north-west London, where we'd been the best of friends. I was no dummy; I knew that my new lease of life owed as much to Carmen's influence as it did to the new furniture in my office.

'How's it going then?'

'Okay . . .' She screwed up her nose, making freckles move and disappear, her expression saying the opposite. 'Did yuh see someone waitin' outside fuh me?'

'I did. I thought he wasn't one of mine.'

'Yeah, that's Mr Oyeyemi. I haven't fully taken him on yet. I just been reviewin' his case. It's scary, Vinnie. Another missin' K-I-D scenario involvin' an African boy. What wiv all dat stuff in the papers about the B-O-D-Y found in the Thames, everybody's scared about ritual K-I-L-L-I-N-G-S. Even West Indian parents. Last week I had Mr Oyeyemi in my office cryin' his eyes out in front of me, right where you're standing. It's so sad.'

'What's a ritual killing?' Akira said, in a light-hearted tone that gave no sign of the seriousness of her words. She knew it meant something bad though. She wouldn't look her mother in the eye and she played with the zipper on her Gap Kids jacket while she waited for an answer. Carmen winced and gave me a look that begged for help. I shrugged.

'I'll tell you when you're older,' she said finally, lifting her daughter from her lap. 'Baby, why don't you go out with Sadie and talk to her for a minute?'

'She might be on the phone,' I told Carmen. 'But you can go on my computer if you want, Akira. I've got some new games you can try.'

'Sure.'

Akira got off her mother's lap and walked from the room with all the poise and grace of a catwalk model. Carmen was watching her go, shaking her head.

'That girl . . .'

'She's gonna get worse you know . . .' I teased,

14

studying her face for a reaction. 'She's already like a little woman.'

'I'm dreading thirteen,' Carmen said, sitting back in her seat with a nervous smile. 'I'm not jokin' either. She's gonna be worse than we were.'

'Worse than you were, you say? Now that's a scary thought.'

I walked over to the desk and kissed Carmen on the forehead, which she accepted by raising her head my way and closing her eyes. I looked down and saw Mr Oyeyemi's file on the computer monitor.

'D'you want me to take a look at that?' I motioned at the computer screen. 'Two heads might be better than one?'

'Yeah sure, if you think you can help out, go ahead. Unless you've got things of your own you'd rather deal with.'

I shrugged and made a sad face. 'Nah, I've got nothing at the minute actually. It's real quiet on my side of the office. I told you you'd take all of my clients one day . . .'

Carmen looked me in the eye to make sure I was joking, blushing bright red and looking at her lap as though searching for traces of her daughter. It was a joke I had made ever since she became my partner three years ago. She squirmed every time I said it. I was testing her, making sure the status quo was still as it had been all that time ago, using her shame as a means of measuring her feelings. I felt slightly mean for acting this way, but I usually couldn't help myself.

'Don't be silly, Vinnie. Everyone goes through quiet spells every now and then.' She was growing more embarrassed by the second. I decided to let her off the hook.

'I know, Carmen. I was joking,' I said, winking in the hope that she'd believe me. 'Print me those files will you. I'd be glad to help.'

TWO

Carmen did as I asked. I took the papers into my office. The details of the case were compelling enough to drown out Akira's bursts of whispering as she played computer games on the internet, and even the sound of Carmen entering the room a few minutes later, telling me she was taking her daughter home. I nodded, my mind distracted, kissing Akira and her mother goodnight. Not long after that, Sadie buzzed me on the intercom to tell me she was also leaving. I kept the conversation to a minimum, answering her queries as best I could, turning back to the file as soon as it was polite to do so.

Mr Oyeyemi's son, Ulla Shola, had been a bright and able boy according to his parents, friends and schoolteachers. He had been a friendly and fairly streetwise child, born and bred in Finsbury Park, north London, well known for his intelligence. He studied hard,

17

had performed very well in his SATs exams and was well respected by his peers.

Exceptional things were expected from Shola when he left the small primary to start secondary school. Then, one day, after the final bell of the day had rung, a man his friends had never seen before met Shola at the school gates. Eye-witness reports described him as a large, heavy black male, as tall as he was round. He greeted Shola with grunts and tugs of his arm instead of hugs and kisses.

When some of the children approached their friend, asking who the man was to him, the adult silenced their questions with harsh words, calling Shola by name and dragging him forcefully towards a silver Ford Mondeo. Other parents saw the incident. Sadly for Shola, none of them knew the child, or his parents. Nobody was sure if they should intervene or not, even though Shola was fighting against the man at that stage. By the time his friends went back into the school building and returned with some teachers, both the child and the Ford Mondeo were gone.

I read the file twice over, sat back, closed my eyes and thought about what those papers contained. I knew enough these days to realise it wasn't that the police and general public didn't care about these kids as much as other missing children. Time and resources were the issue, not race. Missing children were a big problem in inner-city Britain, and like many problems this country faced, it tended to hit black people that much harder, resulting in more disappearances and fewer cases solved. Whatever resources the police and media had were often all used up by the time the black cases came round. Apart from the horrific remains of a child found in the Thames, none of these other cases had made headlines.

I looked at my watch. I'd become so interested in reading the file I hadn't even realised that it was past seven in the evening. Time to go home. I got my coat and locked up, feeling quite weary even though I'd hardly done a solid day's work.

Outside my office I paused, looking at the door beside mine. I became very curious. There was no sign of the pretty East-Asian woman Akira had bumped into that afternoon, although the dark-blue office door she'd disappeared into was half open. I pushed it a little with my fingertips. The door swung open slightly to reveal a reception set-up that was a bit like mine: a waiting area, a desk with a computer, monitor and printer, files in boxes all over the floor. I couldn't stop my feet from taking me further. They pointed me directly towards the files. Before I had even taken three steps a voice came from behind me.

'Can I help you?'

I turned to find the East-Asian woman standing beside an East-Asian man who didn't look too pleased. I looked again, and decided that really, neither of them looked too pleased. No one said anything for a very long time. I felt like a burglar caught mid-creep, with the family jewels in one hand and a torch in the other.

'Hi. I was just looking for you actually,' I said, directing my conversation at the woman in the hope that she would remember me. 'I just wanted to tell you how sorry I was about this morning.'

'Okay.'

We stood there in total silence. I began to grow hot with embarrassment.

'So I'm sorry.'

Nothing. They looked in my face, their own

expressions blank, and waited for me to get out of there.

'Okay, you're obviously busy, so I'll leave you both to get on.'

They nodded, saying nothing more. I moved out of the way to let them walk past and into the office. The door shut behind me with a bang that echoed down the silent, empty corridor.

How weird.

Shaking my head at the strange scene, I left the passageway for home. Funnily enough, even though the Oyeyemi file had been on my mind ever since I had taken it from Carmen, the plight of the little African boy was forgotten on the drive back to my house. Now all I could think about was the blank faces of the man and woman outside that blue office door.

Around a month or so passed. My interest in the office next to ours never went away – in fact I began to think about it a lot. Strange things were happening there, I was sure of it. First came the arrival of two black letters nailed to the dark-blue door, one 'S' and one 'N'. Apart from that, there was nothing else to tell anyone

21

who the company was, or what they did. Most offices in my building had a name tag, stickers or even a graphic-designed logo. My next-door neighbours had two letters.

Second came the fact that I never saw any staff enter or leave that office since the day I'd been caught snooping around. No one. The office block was a large building, with well over four hundred office spaces spread over five floors. I had been renting mine for a number of years and was well used to greeting people from other offices as we all came and went. What with the small corridors and only one main entrance, we couldn't help but bump into each other. But I never saw any staff members go inside or come out of the office next door to mine.

If I had my way I would have set up camp in the cold, bare corridor, waiting to see the East-Asian woman or anyone else that might wander along. I couldn't, of course. Even if I could, I was pretty sure that there would have been nothing to see. No one else noticed any signs of life either – not Sadie and especially not Carmen, who was even nosier than me.

The other thing was the customers that came

there. I'd just got used to the fact that no staff came or went, when a constant flow of people began to go in and out of the dark-blue doors around four days after they moved into the building. They came in such high numbers Sadie wondered if our next-door neighbours were in the business of selling winning lottery tickets at cut price.

The people began to arrive around eight in the morning and kept going way into the middle of the night, from what Manny, our building's janitor, told me. He would have asked questions, Manny went on, if he hadn't been warned against it by his manager, who'd told him they were very tidy, very polite and paid their rent on time. I remember thinking that the old man was advising me not to get too curious.

Whenever I brought up the subject of the office next door, Carmen and Sadie teased me without mercy. They blamed my interest on my attraction to the woman, and were right in a way. Still, although I couldn't convince them otherwise, there was actually a lot more to it. Something didn't feel right about their need for secrecy, lack of advertising and the blank look in the eyes of the man and woman who'd found me snooping. Something felt false about the name she'd given me, Elizabeth, and her body language when she'd said it: eyes down, distant, almost unwilling to tell me anything. Carmen suggested that they might have thought I was a thief, which was true of course. But it didn't explain our first meeting, when the woman couldn't get away fast enough. Something dodgy was going on, I just didn't know what.

Things got really interesting when I came into work one morning, whistling and carrying my usual copies of the *Independent* and the *New Nation* beneath my arm. I had been making my way into the building for my normal 9 a.m. start. I found Sadie in the corridor outside the mysterious office door, staring as though hypnotised. Her forehead was creased. Her huge chest rose and fell as she breathed. She almost looked as though she was meditating. I stood by her side, nudging her arm.

'What's up, Sade?'

'They're gone,' she said at once, not looking my way. 'There's been loads of people knocking their door, even a few knocking ours. No one's answering. They've just packed up and gone.'

'See! I told you something strange was going on in that office,' I moaned, a little put out that no one had believed me. 'You and Carmen should have listened. Now we'll never know what it was.'

Although I was right about the mysterious nature of the company behind the blue door, the second half of my complaint couldn't have been more wrong. A few hours later I was sitting behind my desk making some phone calls when the intercom buzzed.

'Hey, Sadie.'

'Ervine, there's a DS Lindsey and DS Moore here to see you.'

I frowned at the tiny black machine and scratched my head.

'Send 'em through, Sade, it's cool.'

The next thing I knew, two detectives were entering my office. And I'm being serious, it was that quick. They were typical Metropolitan Police material: tall and broad-shouldered, with rugged faces that told me they'd spent a lot of time on the streets as PCs. I respected that, so I stood up when they came in. They introduced themselves. Moore was the bigger one, his short black hair carefully styled and his suit tailor-made, which was no doubt meant to hide the fact that he was as rough as the heel of a tramp's shoe. Lindsey was just as tall as his partner but a great deal thinner. He had wide brown eyes that took in everything around him and a thin smile that told me he'd be difficult to fool.

I offered them a seat on my sofa along with some tea, which they accepted. I buzzed Sadie for the hot drinks, feeling relaxed, knowing they needed something by the uncertain glances they shot at each other. Neither man knew where to begin. It was a great position for me.

'So, what's going on boys?'

Lindsey sat forward a little.

'Well, I'll get straight to the point—'

'Always helpful,' I broke in. There were distant smiles from both.

'Now I know that this is going to sound strange, but you have to hear me out, Ervine . . . We've already spoken to DS Birkett down at Notting Hill before we came. He told us that you're someone we can trust.'

Birkett. He was an old friend of mine from a few years back, someone I'd trust with my life if I had to. I held my hands out, palms towards them, urging Lindsey to continue. I wasn't saying anything more until I knew what they wanted. He recognised that.

'We have reason to believe that the people who rented the office next door to yours have been involved in highly illegal activities. Activities that come with a lengthy jail sentence attached . . .'

I was too excited to sit still.

'I thought so.'

'You did?' Lindsey leaned forward. His nose almost twitched like that of a sniffer dog catching a scent. 'Why?'

I shrugged, remembered my former calm and leaned back in my seat.

'It just seemed a little suspicious over there, that's all.'

'Did you see anything suspicious?'

That was Moore's deeper tone. I shook my head.

'No, not really. It was more like a feeling.'

The men both relaxed a little. Moore went on.

'As you well know, Ervine, we need evidence of any wrongdoing before we can pursue allegations.'

'Of what? Drug dealing or something?'

The policemen laughed a little, then got serious. From my side of the desk it looked something like that game people play, when they pass a hand in front of their face, changing an expression from happy to sad.

'Why did you say that?' Lindsey asked, staring at me with those intent eyes.

'I saw lots of people coming and going, no staff to speak of . . .'

Both nodded as one, heads down so that I could see their bald spots, looking grave. Sadie knocked at the door and came in with the teas. The men looked into their laps while she placed two mugs on my desk in front of them. They nodded and smiled in thanks while I watched them. As soon as she left, Lindsey got back to business.

'I see what you mean, but we don't think they were dealing.'

'Then what?'

Moore cleared his throat and smoothed down his already smooth trousers.

'We happen to believe that the people in that office were involved in a programme of voluntary deaths, Ervine. Allegedly, they were

28

accepting payments for carrying out assisted suicides.'

I didn't know what to say. I assumed something would come to me at some point, so I waited. Time ticked away and nothing did. I even wanted to smile at one point, thinking that this was another joke, waiting for the punchline. One look at their faces told me they were actually serious.

'Do you really believe that?'

'It's what all the evidence suggests,' Moore said, a blank look on his face. 'We've had signed statements from relatives who previously filed missing reports with us, talking about some company called Suicide Note, who they claim are involved in assisted deaths. Of course, in the beginning we laughed it off just as much as anyone. Too much happening in this city without having to listen to some crackpot going on about their brother's suicide being murder, especially with the bombs and all.

'But when you end up drinking with lads from other stations who talk about three different regions where people say the same thing, you start to wonder. When the bodies turn up and you get that tingling feeling in the palms of your hands, and you do interviews with a few relatives where the details start to match, then you begin to doubt your earlier doubts, if you know what I mean.'

'I do,' I said, fully alert. 'My tingles are more around my stomach than the palms of my hands to be honest, but I get where you're coming from.'

Moore and Lindsey smiled at each other. I had a moment to reflect on how different my dealings with the police were now from my days as a youth.

'We need your help with this one, Ervine.'

That was Lindsey. I jumped in my seat, even though part of me had known it was coming.

'Me? Why? You don't need me on this. I thought you would have launched a full investigation, got the Thames Valley boys involved.'

Another silence. Lindsey and Moore each turned a deep shade of red. I looked from one to the other. Their reaction was almost as strange as the goings on in the office next door.

'What's wrong?'

Moore, braver of the two, came out and said it.

'Our superior doesn't actually believe there's enough evidence to support a case, Ervine . . .' He sighed. 'We're here off our own backs, if you know what I mean.'

'Yeah, I know.' I tried to maintain a cheerful nature even though I was feeling a little unhappy. I had already guessed the rest of this story. 'So how do I get paid?'

'Well . . . the relatives of the deceased have clubbed together in order to offer a reward if this thing leads to a conviction,' Moore volunteered, an apology written all over his face.

'How much?'

'Fifteen thousand.'

I closed my eyes, watching the colours come and go, listening to the sounds of their breathing as I thought about that.

'It's not much.'

'I know, Ervine,' Lindsey said, his urgency causing me to open my eyes. 'But the hardest part will be tracking the company down to their new premises. They must be in the process of assisting clients. We've been told they only close up shop and move somewhere else when they're ready to carry out the actual suicides. All

31

you have to do is find them and we'll take it from there. Without any evidence we can't possibly arrest someone, and we can't do it ourselves in case it's thrown out of court purely because our superior won't let us handle this. It'll be seen as police harassment and nothing more, Ervine. We have to stop these people committing more murders.'

'How long have I got to think about it?'

Moore looked at his watch.

'Five minutes.'

I opened my mouth to protest. The burly Detective Sergeant cut me off before I could.

'People are going to *die* if we waste any more time, Ervine. You could do something about it. Think about that.'

'I am,' I replied, returning his blank stare. 'I'll do it.'

They took my agreement well enough. No signs of excitement, only a grim nod as though they'd expected nothing else.

'I take it you have some evidence?'

'Only family statements. I suggest you interview them if only to fill out what's been said.' Lindsey dug into his pocket and produced a USB Flash Key, its casing silver and red, looking a little like a pocket penknife. 'It's all on this. The last woman on the list has a pretty interesting story to tell.'

'Cheers.' I took the USB and plugged it into my computer. While I fiddled with the mouse, clicking windows and opening folders, the two detectives got to their feet.

'Going so soon?

Lindsey sighed, looking more casual now that the business was over with.

'We shouldn't even be here in the first place, Ervine, to tell the truth. If the boss found out we'd both be suspended at the very least, maybe even be out of a job. What I'm saying is, we'd like your secrecy on this one.'

I smiled, noting that it was the first time I'd done this since the detectives had entered my office.

'Of course. I think you'll find that privacy is my middle name . . .'

THREE

Not long after DS's Lindsey and Moore had left my office, Carmen poked her head around the door. I was sitting at my desk, reading the information they had given me, writing down names and addresses of witnesses and family members of the deceased. Although I knew that she was there, I took no notice for a long time, unwilling to break the focus I had developed. I could feel her wanting to ask questions. She watched me write and read for a few moments more, then cleared her throat in greeting. I looked up from my notes.

'Hey. What's going on?'

'Nothing,' she said, making a tired face. 'I was about to ask you the same. Sadie said the police were here earlier.'

'They were.'

'What for? Not been paying your parking tickets?'

'Hardly,' I smiled. 'They just wanted a chat

about something, that's all.'

'I see.' Carmen gave me one of her knowing glances, bright eyes lowered, a glimmer of a smile hidden in the slight curl of her lip. 'Well, you know where I am if you wanna talk about it.'

'I certainly do.'

She disappeared back behind the door, heading for her own office. My tiny smile became a grin. It was always good to have a true friend like Carmen working with me. Since she'd been installed in the little room next to mine the police had also visited her on some confidential business or other, usually cases they needed outside help to solve. I thought back to the days when I'd rebelled against the idea of Carmen being a PI, and I found myself wondering whether I'd been stark raving mad. Her skills came naturally, much of them down to a simple ability to look at a situation as it truly was, rather than as she believed.

I gathered up the notes I'd made, grabbed my phone and other essentials, then left the office, wandering downstairs to the basement. Manny, the building janitor, was in his tiny shoebox of an office, watching a black and white television with no more than a 10-inch screen. CCTV footage was displayed on larger screens all around him. It showed every nook and cranny on every floor of the building. We touched fists. I asked him if he could let me into the office next to mine for five minutes or so, strictly off the record. Manny, whose tall and skinny frame hid powerful physical strength, stretched out his legs and gave me a look very similar to Carmen's knowing stare.

'Anyting to do wid de police dat come visit?'

I held my hand on my heart.

'I cannot tell a lie . . . My lips are sealed. Come on, Manny, you know if it was you I'd help out.'

A few months ago, a young cousin of Manny's had gone missing in south-east London. It had taken a while for Carmen and myself to track her as far as Colchester, where she'd run to with a girlfriend from university. It turned out that they'd been having a secret affair. Although he'd been dismayed at the discovery of his cousin's sexuality, Manny had been more than happy with the service we'd supplied, especially as it had been on the cheap. He'd always said he owed us one. I didn't need to say anything more for him to realise I was calling in the favour.

Upstairs, walking around the empty office it was easy to tell that whoever ran this suicide business was no fool. The space had not only been cleared of the boxes and desks I'd seen, it also smelled of heavy-duty disinfectant, which probably meant that every corner had been thoroughly scrubbed to remove fingerprints. I walked from room to room, hoping that they had slipped up somewhere along the line. The space offered no clues. If I were to make any progress here, it wouldn't be made easy for me. I thanked Manny and left him to lock up. I checked the first name on my list of notes, then headed out into the bright sunshine of the London streets.

Teresa Burrows was a tiny, self-contained woman with long brown hair and a plain face that you wouldn't have looked at twice in passing. Her shoulders were hunched. She wrinkled her nose when she talked, so much so that she reminded me of a little brown mouse. She lived on the St Raphael's Estate in Neasden, a collection of modern council buildings not far from the North Circular Road. Across a small road, just yards from the estate, stood a herd of warehouse-sized superstores.

I hadn't expected Teresa to be inside the house. Everyone seemed to be on the streets making the most of what little summer we might get. I'd knocked on the door of her ground-floor flat, already thinking of moving on to one of the other names on the police files, and was surprised when locks began to click, one after another, like the doors to some ancient tomb. When it opened I was interested but not surprised to see pins and slides pushed deep into her hair and a thick cardigan wrapped tight round her chunky frame. Dark eyes concentrated on every word I said with the hunger of a person craving ordinary, everyday things like speech.

I sat in the lounge while Teresa made tea and brought it out on a plastic tray. The house looked like it hadn't been decorated in a long time. It was spotlessly clean, yet the walls were covered in orange and brown wallpaper with patterns like the shapes formed by lava lamps. There were pictures and statues of Jesus Christ everywhere I turned, alongside scriptures carved into marble books on the mantelpiece. Family photos that seemed to have been taken decades ago took pride of place on the wall. Most seemed like wedding pictures, the men wearing shapeless suits and mullet hairstyles, the women in bright dresses and large hats.

I sat on the sofa, thinking I could feel plastic against my backside. When I looked down I saw it had once been suede and was now so worn it had begun to shine. Teresa sat in a rocking chair across the room from me, cardigan buttoned, thick knees placed together as firmly as two bricks in a wall. She hugged a Charles and Diana Royal Wedding mug to her chest. I accepted the tea and asked about her brother, Mitchell.

'Mitchell . . .' Teresa sighed. She didn't say any more for quite a while, and held her head down so that her hair fell around her face. I waited, watching.

'He was such a good man,' she said at last, her voice as low as her self-confidence. Her vocal chords seemed dry, as if a long time had passed since she'd last used them. Each word seemed like a struggle.

'Mitch had his problems of course . . . He

couldn't help 'em though. They was passed from our father, who got 'em from his mother, who probably got 'em from her father too, for all I know. He tried to fight it, but he couldn't. It was in the bloodline.'

'What kind of problems?' I asked, although I already knew from her files.

'Mental issues,' Teresa said, smiling. Her teeth were as yellow as one-pound coins. It was a grin that was wide and emotionless at the same time, like that of a circus clown. I glanced at the walls and took another sip of milky tea.

'I see . . . And how badly did these issues affect Mitchell?'

'Oh, you can call him Mitch,' she told me, nodding her head. 'He liked people calling 'im that. Made him feel *cool*, I think.'

It's amazing how much the word cool actually sounds like it feels. I hadn't thought about it until that moment. Watching Teresa's lips say the word with such satisfaction brought this home to me.

'Okay, I will. So could you tell me how these issues affected your brother?'

'Oh a lot. . . . They affected 'im a great deal.'

'In what ways?'

She shuffled in her seat, a little uncomfortable now. Her sight line fell into her mug of tea.

'Mitch was in and out of a lotta hospitals. Our father had been too, but Mitch was a lot worse an' he resented Dad for not giving him a normal life. See Dad was so far gone he couldn't ever really come back. Was trapped in his own mind they told us. Hospital was the best place for him they said. Mitch, on the other hand, had months of real clear moments, loadsa times where he knew exactly what had happened to him, when and why. If he was here now he would've been able to sit down wiv us, drink his cup of tea an' tell you all about his illness in detail – the clinical explanation, the treatments he was gettin', everything. Mitch was right clever like that, Mr James, much too clever I reckon. I think he knew too much about his condition for his own good.'

'So what happened? With Suicide Note I mean.'

'Well, I'm not sure, Mr James—'

'Ah, it's Ervine actually. You can call me Ervine.'

She smiled another gold-coloured grin.

41

'Thanks.' A pause while she sucked up more tea. 'Like I was saying anyway, I'm not sure what exactly happened. First I recall was when Mitch started going on about his condition. He'd always had a lot to say on the subject if you know what I mean, but this was more than usual. All of a sudden, you know, he seemed to have lost hope. There didn't look like there was any way to get it back. His social worker, Jane Simmons she was, ever such a lovely girl too. She even come round one or twice when she wasn't meant to. She tried to talk to us and find out what was really going on.'

'What did you think was going on?'

'At the time I thought it was his condition gettin' worse. That's what Jane seemed to think too, cos he started sayin' all this stuff about "when his time comes" and "he ain't got long to go". Scary stuff that made me want to cry. He started going church, not jus' Sundays either. He'd go Tuesdays, Wednesdays, Thursdays an' Fridays too. He started on about God an' Jesus Christ almost as much as his condition.

'Now don't get me wrong, Mitch wasn't one ah those anti-religious blokes or nuffin', he'd jus' never taken much notice of the church before. I'd go every Sunday, but he never came wiv me . . . Now he was goin' more than the bloomin' vicar. I says, "Aye, aye – something's not quite right over here."'

Listening to Teresa Burrows, I could have said the same thing. She laughed a long and loud cackle, sounding a little like a pantomime witch. In the middle of long speeches her eyes would dart around the room. She seemed to have a lot of nervous twitches and tics. I became very aware of the lack of air in the room, how hot the tea was making me, and of course, Teresa Burrows. The mental illness that had caused her father and brother's condition had definitely affected her own mind, although she seemed to be dealing with a much milder version.

'So what happened then?'

'I found this in Mitch's room . . .'

She leaned towards me holding a sky-blue business card, only this one had no name and address printed on the front or back, only two words – SUICIDE NOTE – together with a local landline telephone number. I took the card and turned it over between my fingers.

'It was lyin' on his bed with some papers. I

43

looked through them to see what was what. It was a contract sayin' Mitch was legally bound to suicide. He'd paid this company over five grand to do it. It was signed and everything too. I was so upset I couldn't believe it was true. I said something to him about it that night, told him to get his money back and make them stop. He went mad, sayin' I'd been sneakin' around in his things, I had no right, people like me made him sick. Then he was gone, out of the house without any bags or clothes or anything.

'That night I was on the phone ringin' some people that knew him when I heard a funny noise from his room. Shufflin' or somethin', like mice. I put down the phone, went over to Mitch's room an' opened the door an' I swear on my father's grave there was someone in there. I know it was dark and I couldn't really see proper, but you know when another person's in the same room as you, don't you? You don't need eyes to see that do you, Ervine?'

'I wouldn't have thought so.'

'Well, I didn't either. I was so scared I screamed for about two minutes straight and when I switched on the light there was no one there. The room was a mess and the window

44

was open a little, so that must have bin how they got in, don't you reckon? I do.

'Four days later they found Mitch in the Grand Union Canal. Drowned. They said he jumped. I don't think so. They said they found the note, pills and everything in a little rucksack not far from where they pulled him out of the water. I wanted to show 'em the contract and card but they weren't with the bag and I couldn't find them for ages. Mitch musta took 'em, that's what I thought. Now I reckon that's what that intruder was looking for – the contract innit? It never turned up, but I found that card under his bed when I was clearing out the room a few months ago. So I told the police about it. They says it wasn't enough evidence an' left it at that. The only one who believed me was Jane Simmons. She left the job a few weeks after Mitch died. I ain't seen her since. Fat lotta good she was.'

'She must've felt bad about what happened.'

'Not as bad as me.'

There was no answer to that.

'You're lucky you found this card. Whoever told you it wasn't enough evidence was probably too lazy to chase it up. We can use

45

this, Teresa, it's a good thing you held on to it.'

She looked up at me sharply, like a pleased child receiving praise for the first time. Her face lit up. I was moved.

'I did well?' she asked, almost begging me to say yes.

'Yes you did, Teresa. It was very clever of you.'

She rocked back and forth in her seat and nodded to herself.

'So where did your brother get the money to pay these people five grand, Teresa?'

'Benefits, mostly,' she replied. 'He never used to spend it on much, so he had a load saved an' stuff. He even still had a few grand left when he died. I was gonna get his name engraved on a park bench until it all got spent on funeral expenses.'

'I'm sorry.'

She looked up from her mug. The glow in her eyes had faded and they were blank again. Her cheeks twitched a little, although they never gave.

'That's all right. I was upset when it happened but it was a long time ago now, over eighteen months. Time is the master they reckon, an' I believe 'em. You can grieve for a

46

while and then you jus' hafta get on, right?'

I smiled back at her, meaning it this time.

'You're a very brave woman, Teresa. An' I'll have you know that the police came to me to see if I could help, so some of them do believe you. We're gonna do all we can to find your brother's murderer.'

'They did it,' Teresa said, pointing at the card. Her eyes were blind, void of emotion. She put down the Royal Wedding mug and rested a hand on her heart. 'I can feel it right here,' she told me, and closed her eyes.

The first thing I did when I left Teresa's house was put a call in to Moore and Lindsey. Moore answered after the first ring, his deep voice rumbling in my ear, wondering how things were going. I read out the phone number on the sky-blue card and asked him to pester BT to find out who the number was registered to. It was a bit more work than Moore thought he'd have to do, yet he was willing enough. He promised to have an answer by the afternoon, and cracked lame jokes about getting paid overtime.

Just before he ended the call, Moore asked me what I thought of Teresa Burrows. It took a while to come up with an answer. Eventually, I settled for telling him that I thought she was a sad and lonely woman. I was thinking about what I'd said as I rang off and unlocked my car doors. I wondered if the kind of solitude Teresa Burrows had was really such a bad thing.

FOUR

I checked the name above Teresa's on the information I'd printed from the police files and pointed the car in that direction. The address was in Fulham and traffic seemed quite heavy today. I settled back and prepared for a long drive. On the way I gave the number on the sky-blue card a call. After some seconds I got an engaged tone, loud in my ear. Great. I'd hoped it would be easier than that. Teresa had done well to hold on to the card, yet if I couldn't get through to anyone and Moore couldn't use his contacts to track down the owner of the number, I'd be left with nothing.

Even though Teresa had told me all the details she could remember, the policeman she'd spoken to all those months ago had been half-right. None of it amounted to a scrap of real evidence. The other interviews were unlikely to reveal any more information, especially if the police had already visited the friends and family of victims. There was no one to even arrest, let alone bring to trial, and nothing to say that Mitchell hadn't just jumped into the Grand Union Canal of his own will, just like everyone seemed to think.

I thought some more about Mitchell. I tried to imagine life getting so bad that I'd feel like jumping into the mossy green water of an ancient canal. Earlier, when Moore and Lindsey had told me about this case, I'd promised myself that I'd be professional and not make a judgement about the rights and wrongs of people taking their own lives. It wasn't that I disagreed with it as such. I just couldn't imagine why or how someone would become so unhappy that they would actually try to harm themselves.

The image came to me as soon as I let it. A tall, broad man with deep-set eyes, standing at the canal bank, looking into the dark water and taking deep breaths. His hands are clenching and unclenching by his sides. His face is grim and free of expression. His mind is already flown far from his body. Knees bending a little, his feet push from the concrete. I imagined the splash as he enters, the cold feeling seeping up to his legs, his groin, his stomach, across his chest and neck and then over his mouth, the water thick and sticky like cough syrup. I pictured his first attempted breath, the water rewarding Mitch with a taste of moss, sharp and like nettles . . .

I had to pull the car over and did it quickly, while motorists behind me beeped long blasts of anger. I waved them by and edged my Audi up on to a curb, sitting there breathing heavily. That was why I never let my imagination take control. I became a passenger along for the ride, open to nightmare images and emotions. Usually it showed me the past, events that could have happened beside others that actually did, each one as bloody and terrifying as the next.

I cursed myself beneath my breath as I took a deep lungful of air. Who was I trying to kid with my silly games? I was no ordinary man. I would do well to remember that. I was somebody who had seen war and horror, who had seen friends killed yards from my side and who had killed too. I had taken part in a conflict history would like to forget, and received no thanks, even less regret. I should stop trying to test myself with games that were built for stronger minds.

Would I ever have committed suicide? It was fine to be smug about it at this stage of my life, to square my shoulders and say it would never happen, but that was a lie. In the past, way before my big job, in fact long before I'd had any job at all, when I was more or less a young kid fresh from the Falklands with no future prospects and a head full of hell-sent memories, I had often thought about suicide.

I'd planned a much easier route. Put my service revolver in my mouth and pull the trigger. Simple as that. No contracts, no money, no outside help. Five thousand pounds was a lot of money to a person with no hope. Or maybe it was like five pence? Whatever the reality, it would be hypocritical of me to object to the belief that human beings had the right to take their own life. A company that made profit from others' bad luck was another thing entirely.

I sat back in the driver's seat with my eyes closed thinking the whole thing over, when my mobile rang. I looked at the caller ID. It was Sadie in the office so I let the hands-free answer.

'Ervine, it's me.'

'I know, Sade, I've got caller ID remember? How you doing anyway?'

'I'm okay, I'm okay . . .'

'What's going on?'

'I've had Tanya on the phone three times in the last half hour, talking about you were supposed to meet her and your brother at some restaurant.'

'Shit!'

It was the truth. I had been planning to meet Dougie and his girlfriend Tanya at Cotton's Caribbean restaurant for over two weeks. I knew that it was Suicide Note that had made me forget, but my brother didn't. He was so sensitive he would take my no-show as a sign of disrespect. If I didn't go and make up with him I'd be risking an already troubled relationship.

'Tell me about it,' came Sadie's casual reply. 'You gonna go then?'

'I have to, Sade.'

'Want me to call Tanya and let her know?'

'Would you? Apologise for me and tell her I'll be half an hour tops. And get her to make Dougie wait, yeah?'

'No worries.'

I breathed a mental sigh of relief that soon turned real.

'Thanks, Sade!'

'It's what I'm paid for innit? See you later, love.'

'Later.'

I sat upright and looked around at the other cars. Maybe half an hour was pushing it from here, though I could just make it if I took back roads. Starting the Audi up, I slipped into the afternoon traffic, heading north again.

Cotton's Caribbean restaurant was just a bus ride away from Camden Town, and had been a firm favourite of mine for many years. Before the Walker case, going there had been a method of treating myself, of keeping my spirits up if I'd worked for a year or more without ending up in severe debt. Nowadays visits came at least once a month, sometimes even more.

The restaurant was brightly decorated although under-lit, the walls painted dark red, reminding me of blood that ran through the deepest veins. Huge oil paintings of island life were hung wherever I looked: faceless characters caught in mid-dance; a woman selling coconuts; a group of men 'liming' by a street corner on a hot afternoon, drinking cold beers. Cotton's waitresses were European and cheerful, the decor and fittings mostly dark wood, varnished until everything gleamed.

I walked in, ordered a brandy and Coke from the bar and climbed a short set of stairs towards some tables at the back. Peter Tosh's 'Legalise It' was playing on the stereo. Although I hardly agreed with the idea, I sang along for a couple of bars. Tanya, my brother's live-in girlfriend, was sitting at one of the tables looking bored, smoking a cigarette. She was as pretty as a hip hop video girl: light-skinned, round cat-like face, deep almond-shaped eyes, rosy lips and a body that made most men look twice, just in case they never got a chance to see it again. Needless to say, she wasn't my type.

My younger brother Dougie had always been more than a little streetwise for my liking and his taste in women reflected that. Still, there was something about my brother's girlfriend that I couldn't help admiring, despite the fact that she reminded me of a younger Carmen without the charm. If you looked up 'classy' in the dictionary, I was sure you would see Tanya's face looking up from the page without a trace of a smile, eyes blank, lips a dark, thin line. She genuinely seemed not to give a damn about anything but stayed fully committed to my brother and the foolishness he got up to.

Tanya and Dougie had been going out together since their late teens. They rented a flat two years ago and both seemed to enjoy living the common-law life. Despite my brother's wayward nature on many counts, his bad behaviour never seemed to stretch to cheating. Tanya loved Dougie and the same was true for my brother. I'd always been sure of that.

I smiled as I approached her. She managed an expressionless lift of both cheeks, which disappeared as fast as it came. I bent over the table to kiss one side of her face. At the last moment she turned her head so her lips pressed quickly against mine. She smelt of cocoa butter and Aveda hair products, as well as some other perfumed smell that I couldn't quite place. I stood up and looked her in the eye to see what that was all about. She was already focusing past me for a waitress, one slim hand raised to chin height.

'Hi, Tanya. How are you?'

'I'm cool,' she said, still looking over my shoulder. 'How are you?'

'I'm fine. Sorry I'm late by the way, I got caught up with some stuff.' I sat down, realising there was no jacket on the back of the chair next to Tanya's. 'Where's Dougie?'

She exhaled, a harsh outward breath. A tiny smoke cloud floated across the table as if powered by a gentle breeze. She shrugged.

'Dunno.'

'What d'you mean you don't know? Have you guys been arguing again?'

'Nah, not at all. It ain about arguin' or nuttin', Vinnie. I jus' dunno where my man is.'

She seemed like a little girl at that moment, all lost and lonely. I was studying her with so much concentration I could feel the tension just above my eyelids. I tried to force myself to calm down.

'But we planned this and everything, Tanya.'

'I know.'

I warned myself not to get too self-righteous, especially after my slip-up, although it was still pretty tough. The waitress, a cute skinny girl in a Cotton's promotional T-shirt, appeared by my side.

'Would you like to order?'

I looked at Tanya. She made a face of apology.

'I already ordered a starter, but it ain come yet. You go ahead.'

'Do you do ackee and saltfish to start?'

'Yes we do.'

'I'll have that, thank you.'

'And would you like to look at the menu for a main course, sir?' The waitress smiled.

'Yes please.'

She left the table. I shook my head in anger, letting my frustration show. Tanya watched me fume, looking like a statue.

'What's going on, Tanya? Everyone in the family complains I'm never there, that I'm always working too hard to have time for them. When I make the time they waste it and leave me feeling like a fool. I cancelled appointments for this you know. I moved things around to be here and my brother doesn't even have the decency to let me know he's not coming, let alone consider the fact that I might be upset if he doesn't turn up.'

I was looking into her eyes as I ranted away, sure that my words would be ignored. Yet slowly, bit by bit, Tanya's ice-cold expression began to slip. It was so gradual I wouldn't have even seen it if I wasn't watching so closely. When it did, I had to force myself to blink back surprise. First her left eye began to twitch, ever so slightly. Then the fingers holding the cigarette began to shake and grow nervous as she picked restlessly at the few items on the varnished table: a box of Cottons matches, the golden packet of twenty B&H, the glass ashtray and the red table napkin beside her cutlery. After that she couldn't hold my gaze any longer. Her eyes began to flutter, like hummingbird wings. Her chin dropped into her chest. Her butter complexion grew dark red like the walls. She was biting her lip as though her mind wanted to tell me things her mouth wouldn't dare.

I looked at Tanya for a long time, saying nothing, allowing the pity to seep through my body, together with the feeling that it was not her fault. For all her bravado and attitude, she was still a sensitive young woman, as human and vulnerable as the rest of us.

I reached over the table and held her hand. I don't even know why. The gesture was way beyond our usual boundaries of contact, yet I did it anyway and she didn't pull her hand from mine, so I must have done the right thing. She wouldn't look up. I didn't do anything about that though – I was surprised enough just to have her hand in mine.

'Tanya?' I waited a beat, took a deep breath, and went for it. 'Tanya, what's wrong?'

'It's Dougie.'

'I know it's Dougie. Can you tell me what he's done?'

She sighed, blinking at the table. The waitress came back with the drinks and starters, doing her best not to notice our joined hands. Tanya waited for her to leave before she spoke up.

'Well, you know he got that job at London Transport, right?'

'Yeah.'

It had happened not long after they moved into the flat. After weeks of interviews, Dougie got a night-shift job with the underground service, working with men who took care of track maintenance long after the last train stopped running. I had been surprised and admired his ability to do such work, especially when he stuck at it.

'He got sacked. Three weeks ago.'

Oh well. I tried to keep a neutral look on my face.

'What happened?'

'He wouldn't tell me the whole story. Jus dat some of the guys used to boy him off an' he got tired of it.'

'Boy him off?' Now the news had sunk in, I could feel my poise slipping ever so slightly, a little like Tanya's own control moments before. I took another deep breath. 'What's that supposed to mean?'

She shrugged and let go of my hands.

'You know, like push him around, order him to do all the shitty work . . . I dunno exactly what, I'm just guessin' from the little bits he told me y'get me? Whatever happened, Dougie kept telling me he couldn't take it, the people or the work I mean. I kept saying he should stick at it and not let them get him down. Then all of a sudden he came home with a massive bruise on his forehead talking about how he got into a fight with one other guy there and they ended up nearly knockin' each other senseless. After that I suppose there was nothing else for the foreman to do but sack the both ah dem. So he did.'

'Well that's just great,' I said, flopping back in my seat. 'So what's he doing now?'

'Nothing.'

'Nothing?'

She nodded with vigour, eyes locking on mine. They were round, chestnut brown and very deep.

'So how do you guys pay rent?'

'Tell me about it. I'm still workin' and it's me one bringin' in all the money. It was cool for the first couple of weeks, now I'm startin' to struggle. Dougie's tryin' to get another job, I give 'im dat, he ain exactly sittin' on his arse, but den he ain givin' it one hundred percent either.'

'How d'you mean?'

'It's like, he'll get up an' I'll give him a paper to look at for work. Then I'll leave the house. He'll circle a whole heap ah jobs, phone the first three an' not get nowhere, then give up an' go out wiv his mates. He won't come back till like two in the mornin'. It's not like I'm tryin' to keep him in the house or make him stay away from his bredrins or nuttin' either, Vinnie. There was a time when both of us woulda bin out dere doin' the same stuff yuh nuh? But

62

we're old now man. I'm twenty-seven, he's goin' on twenty-seven himself an' I don't really understand why he thinks he can get away wiv dis shit while I'm out dere workin' like his mother.'

'Do you need money?'

She gave me that hard look again. I returned her gaze, not wanting her to think there was any hesitance or pretence lurking in my offer. I meant what I said. I would help both her and my brother if I had to. I could certainly afford it. Even though I knew I was doing the right thing for the right reasons, there was still something in her eyes that made me feel unsure. I couldn't put my finger on what it was exactly – just a jangling of nerves that occurred every now and then throughout my life. It was a feeling much like the sensation of my teeth being set on edge by a cold object. Only this time it felt like sharp tingles taking place all over my body. I was so busy thinking I hardly noticed Tanya's hand slip back into my own, squeeze twice, then slide back to her side of the table.

'Thanks, Vinnie. I don't think dat's a good idea though. You could only do it for a month or so, then we'd have to find some other way of coverin' t'ings, and we'd be in debt to you too. Money and family don't mix, trust me, I've been there before.'

I nodded, knowing she made sense, even managing to smile.

'Do you want me to have a word with Dougie then?'

'If you think it might make a difference, why not? I know yuh busy though, so if you can't don't worry about it. I'll try and sort suttin' out.'

'I'll talk to him. It might not be right away, but I'll definitely talk to him. It's a promise. After all, like you said, we're family, right?'

Tanya's head jerked up and she looked at me hard once again. This time her eyes were thin slits, and there were crinkles at the edges. I was stunned. Joy made her look five years younger. It made her look beautiful.

'We are innit?' she grinned, picking up her cutlery. 'Let's eat, yeah?'

I wasn't about to argue with that.

FIVE

The waitress was at our table just asking about dessert when my mobile rang. Tanya gave me a 'here we go again' look. I didn't recognise the number but answered anyway. It was DS Lindsey. He had a registered address for the landline number on the sky-blue card. Rogers, Parks and Justin were based just past the Holloway Road, further to the north of London. The phone number was registered under the name Hamish Parks. I scribbled it all down in my notebook, thanked the DS and rang off.

Tanya was looking at me with that blank expression again. The waitress glanced between the two of us with a half smile on her face, as though we were at war and she couldn't wait for the fireworks. I put my pen and notebook away, nervous even though I knew that I had no cause to be.

'I suppose yuh gonna go den?'

Her voice was as emotionless as her face, yet

there was a hint of displeasure present in Tanya's general behaviour that was difficult to mistake.

'I've got no choice, Tanya. It's a work thing and I've got to deal with it.'

'This is what Dougie complains about though, you know dat innit? You always puttin' work first.'

'I know, and as soon as this job is done I'll make it up to the both of you. After he's made it up to me for not being here.'

The waitress waved a hand and said that she'd be back in five minutes. All of a sudden, Tanya began to smile.

'God, you two man, I dunno which brother is worse. No wonder yuh mum just wipes her hands of the whole thing. Must do her head right in.'

'Must do . . .'

I got up from my seat, leaned over the table and made to kiss Tanya's cheek. She turned again so I caught the corner of her mouth this time, grabbing my hand in one of her own and holding it for a moment. She closed her eyes for a tiny second, patted my hand and let go.

'Okay. Go an' save the world, Ervine James. Make sure you call us when yuh done.'

I chuckled a little until I realised she didn't seem to be joking.

'I will.'

I waved once and walked towards the exit. The waitress was standing by the bar, whispering to a barman as I walked by. They stopped and watched me leave as though I was exiting stage left at the theatre.

The address was just off the Highbury and Islington end of Holloway Road, which was quite an easy drive from Camden. I set off trying not to think about Tanya and how well we got on these days. She'd grown into a mature and positive woman. When I'd first met her, around three years ago, Tanya had seemed as wild as an alley cat, a young girl with lots of potential and no drive or ambition to fuel it.

Nowadays she seemed to have shed her 'bad girl' image for one that suited her more, developing a worldly-wise attitude that I respected a lot. I could only wish that Dougie and Maya, my younger brother and sister, could do the same for themselves. It would relieve me no end to see those two pull themselves together like Tanya had.

I'd already guessed the company I was about to visit was either a solicitor's or some kind of agency, so when I pulled up it was no surprise to see a smart office block with the firm's name imprinted on every window. I parked and got out, looking the building over.

A broad man in black trousers and a pink shirt was smoking a cigarette while gazing at the pavement just beyond the doors. As I passed his spot, he flinched and looked up as though shaken from his thoughts. I nodded. He nodded back and looked at the concrete again. If I could remain that unimportant throughout the rest of my PI career, I'd live to become a very happy man.

At the reception I gave my name and asked to see Hamish Parks. The young man at the desk told me he was very busy today and asked if I'd made an appointment. I told him no, although I stressed that I wasn't leaving the building until I'd spoken to Hamish. The young man asked what business I had with Mr Parks. At that point, I have to admit, I lost my temper a little bit. I told him it was police business that could only be discussed with Mr Parks. The young receptionist looked me in the eye for a very long time. I returned the stare, telling him that if I left now I would be back tomorrow with a vanload of officers.

The young man told me to take a seat. I did as I was told and waited ten minutes, watching the guy outside with the cigarette pace and mutter to himself like the drunks you sometimes see on housing estates. He seemed to be lighting one cigarette after another. The kid on reception ignored him, so I guessed he was used to the man's whispered chatter.

I looked at the floor, the paintings and the plants that lined the windows so that no one could see inside the building. I picked up a few magazines from a metal coffee table. Eventually the receptionist told me to go up to the first floor where Mr Parks would be waiting. I gave him a very sarcastic thank you and called the lift without looking back.

When the lift doors opened a young woman was waiting. She was plain, with big blue eyes, thick-rimmed glasses and a head full of Teresa-Burrows-style hairslides. An iPod Shuffle was hanging from her neck like an oversized locket. She didn't smile or even say hello. She simply beckoned me with a finger and led me through office cubicles until we got to a glass-walled room in a far corner.

The girl held a finger up and pressed it against her lips. I nodded, swallowing my smile. She knocked on the glass door and waited. Moments later, a male voice shouted for us to come in. The girl stepped in front of me, opened the door and introduced me to Hamish Parks.

He was a strange-looking man, small and compact like an action figure. He couldn't have been more than five feet five. His limbs were skinny as a sparrow's and he was mostly bald, except for a thin line of hair that went around the sides and back of his head like Jesus Christ's crown of thorns. He wore beige trousers and a white shirt with the sleeves rolled up to his elbow.

From the minute I walked into that room it was easy to tell that Hamish Parks wasn't happy to see me. The fact that I was black didn't seem to impress him much either. He rolled his leather chair back on its wheels and regarded me with eyes that were green and wide and took no shit from anybody. He waved a hand. The girl that had brought me into the room spun on her heel and was gone before I even had time to notice. I looked around for a seat, seeing as I hadn't been offered, and took the nearest I could find.

'I don't remember saying that you could sit, Mr James.'

The man's upper-class accent, along with his rudeness, brought back memories of the Army sergeants in my Gloucestershire training camp, whose life mission had seemed to be the complete breakdown of my emotional and physical defences. I gave him the steady look I had practised for just those occasions. It hadn't been used for many a year.

'That's right, Mr Parks, you didn't. I figured that if I waited to be offered I'd be standing all night, so I decided to take what I wanted.'

Hamish Parks gave me a long cold look and shrugged.

'I suppose I shouldn't expect anything better from your kind.'

'Do you know, I was just thinking the same thing. Call me ridiculous if you like, but I do keep trying. You could say I'm an optimist in that way.'

He didn't know what to say to that. I suppose he thought I'd just get mad and lose it. I wondered how many black men he'd met in real life, instead of behind his desk, in courtrooms and on TV screens.

'So what is it that you want from me?'

'Just a brief chat, Mr Parks. About this.'

I brought the Suicide Note business card from my inside pocket and handed it to Hamish Parks. He looked at it for a while, turning it over between his fingers like a jeweller studying a rare diamond. When he was finished he put the card down on the desk in front of him.

'What's this got to do with me? I've never seen it before in my life.'

'Could I have the card back please, Mr Parks?'

He tried not to let his anger show, unable to stop his face from reddening as he handed the business card back. *Nice try*, I thought, reminding myself to watch his every move.

'Like I said, Mr James, what has that card got to do with me?'

'The landline number is registered to this address. I want to know what links you have to the company named on this card. Otherwise, where you think they might have got this address from.'

Another cold stare. Hamish Parks grew redder until he resembled the devil himself. He was fuming so hard I swear I saw steam coming from his ears. I watched him take deep breaths, trying to get back under control.

'Could I see some ID, Mr James?'

Shit. Back in the day I'd had a fake ID made up by a friend of mine that ran a printing firm. I'd been caught out whenever I showed it to any police officers, so I'd be amazed if it would fool a solicitor. I also had a strong guess that that wasn't the kind of ID he was talking about. I thought back to what I'd said to the young reception guy on the ground floor. *Police business.* I should have known I was setting myself up for trouble the moment those words left my lips.

'Pardon?' I stalled.

'I'd like to see some ID before we go any further with this interview. What are you, a Detective Sergeant, Detective Inspector? What branch do you represent, Holloway Road, Highbury?'

73

Hamish Parks was smiling now, watching me sweat, waiting for the reply that he knew would never come. I stood up. This interview was officially over.

'I'm a private investigator, Mr Parks. I've been asked to look over this case and before you say anything else, I'll have you know that I'm fully backed by the police. If it takes them to come down here to get you to talk, then they'll do it. You better believe they will.'

The devilish grin on Hamish's face only got wider.

'Then if you don't mind, I'd rather wait for the real detectives to arrive before I say anything further to the likes of you. Oh, and before you exit my building I'd just like to ask one thing – have you ever thought of a change of career? You're not a very believable private investigator if you don't mind me saying. I certainly never took you seriously. If you think about it for a moment, though I'm guessing you haven't, there's not much call for your line of work in today's world of modern policing, what with forensics, DNA testing and the like. It doesn't exactly leave you with much room to play with, does it, Mr James? I'm sure there are

74

plenty of other jobs you could perform with much more success. Retail assistant? Street sweeper perhaps? Hmm?'

I smiled at Hamish Parks and decided to ignore him. Being graceful in defeat was something that had always been important to me, and no amount of baiting was about to change that, even if I was fighting the urge to leap over his wide red mahogany desk and beat his face against the surface until both cracked. I believed that I was better than that.

'Thank you for your time,' was all I allowed myself to say, before I turned my back and walked out of the office. I closed his door gently behind me even though I wanted to slam it so hard it smashed into a million pieces. I continued past the office cubicles, avoiding everyone's stares, and took the fire exit, way too embarrassed to wait for the lift.

I was annoyed as well, mostly at myself. What had I expected from that encounter, a signed confession? I knew the man worked the law and yet I'd still walked into his office without any real evidence behind me and expected him to roll over like a playful puppy. It was stupid, that's what it was, plain stupid. Although I thought I'd made all my inexperienced mistakes three years ago on my big case, I'd just been reminded that there was always room for one more. That mistake could happen at any time, just waiting to catch you out if you let it.

I stepped into the lobby and avoided the receptionist, going quickly towards the swing doors. The chain-smoking guy in the pink shirt was sitting in the chair I'd left only minutes earlier. His head was down almost between his legs. When he heard the shuffle of my feet, he shot up and began to grin like a maniac. I was a little stunned by his reaction, so I kept walking and tried to ignore him. Chain-smoker got up from his seat and almost ran across the lobby floor. When he got to my side he tugged my arm, forcing me to stop.

'Yeah?' I said, not feeling much like conversation.

'Are you the police?'

'Sort of . . . but not exactly.'

Chain-smoker grinned a tobacco-stained smile of joy.

'Did you . . . did you just go upstairs to see Hamish Parks?'

'Yeah . . .' My brow was creased like brown

paper. I was still walking towards the swing doors, though at a much slower pace than before. 'Why, do you know anything about what he might be involved in?'

'Do I . . .' The man almost jumped up and down on the spot. He whispered *'Yes!'* beneath his breath, before looking towards the reception desk. The young man was sitting with his hand on the phone receiver watching our conversation through narrow eyes. Chain-smoker took my elbow in one sweat-dampened palm. 'Let's go somewhere we can talk in private. I know the perfect place.'

SIX

The tiny, greasy-spoon café wasn't too far from the Rogers, Parks and Justin offices. At first I had been wary of this, sure that other workers might be found drinking tea or eating bubble 'n' squeak in a corner. Chain-smoker assured me that they all went to a coffee shop around the block that was a lot more upmarket than this. When I looked around the café everybody seemed to fall into one of three categories – bin men, pensioners or building-site workers.

I relaxed a little and observed the man sitting opposite me. He ordered two teas with a child-like enthusiasm and lit another cigarette with a gold-plated lighter. He was tall, though not as tall as myself. I put him at just under six feet. He was quite wide and a lot bigger than Hamish Parks, with thick, hairy arms, broad shoulders and a head that was as large as a basketball. I recognised the cut of his pink shirt as an Ozwald Boateng, and not from a few years ago either – it looked brand new. He smoked without looking at me, urgent puffs that quickly made the end of the cigarette shrivel into white ash. He didn't say a word until the waitress came back with the teas. Then he smiled up at her, said thank you, stubbed his cigarette into a pub ashtray and took the biggest swallow of a hot drink I had ever seen anyone gulp down in my whole life. I had a look in his mug while he blew smoke away from me. Over half of the steaming tea was gone.

'So which one are you then?' I began, strangely comfortable with this odd man. 'Rogers or Justin?'

Chain-smoker looked into my eyes. His were wide, brown and as round as two-penny coins. They made me take a second look at his cigarette just to make sure it was the legal kind.

'You're not that bad at this detective lark, are you?' he said, looking even more cheery. 'How'd you work that one out?'

'I bet there's not many people in that company that can take half-hour cigarette breaks and still go home with a job. Especially with Hamish running the place. That Boateng shirt and the lighter didn't help either.'

'And there I was thinking I was a man of the people. Smoke?'

He offered me the packet.

'Sure.'

I took it and lit up. When I put the lighter down his outstretched hand was waiting.

'Brian Rogers.'

'Ervine James. So what can I do for you, Brian?'

He frowned and looked at the cutlery.

'Carter said that you were with the police, no?'

'The reception guy?' Brian nodded. 'Not exactly. I'm a private investigator. I was interested in finding out why the phone number on this card was registered under your business partner's name.'

I held the sky-blue card up so that Brian could see it. He reached out to take it from me and I pulled back. The card had already done its work. Besides, the man sitting opposite me was nowhere near becoming a suspect in my eyes. He shook his head and looked down at the table.

'I need the police for this. It's the only way to get to that man, the police. A PI just won't do.'

I was hurt and didn't even know why, though I tried not to let it show.

'Well, I am working very closely with police officers on this case. I'm sure I can let them know of any worries you might have if you could just help me out with this number.'

He sat back in the chair, his fingers drumming on the tabletop.

'He's an evil man that one. A racist and thief he is, with no regard for human life. He needs to be stopped.'

'We can try, Brian. With the help of your information, we can try . . .'

'I'm not like him, you know, Ervine. Got two black kids I have, two little girls. Eight and five they are. Been married to a Jamaican woman for the last ten years, real Jamaican too, not this Black British crap. From Clarendon she is, born and raised. I bring my kids into that office and the bastard doesn't even look at them, let alone talk to them. He's a racist through and through. I'm not like that. Half my bloody family's black so I could never be like that pathetic man.'

'Okay . . .'

'Just so you know the truth, right, Ervine? Not all white men are like that.'

'I know. I know that, Brian.' It wasn't that I didn't appreciate his words, but I was starting to question Brian's sanity. 'So, what can you tell me about this number?'

He took another huge gulp of tea and the rest of the mug's contents disappeared. I tried to ignore what I'd seen and to listen to what he had to say.

'Yeah, he's linked to Suicide Note . . .'

'Hamish is, you mean? There is a link?'

'A very long time ago Hamish was best buddies with a guy called Clifford Grantham. I think they went to University together. When Clifford eventually got married and had a child, Hamish was made godfather. She was a little girl named Toby. They were very close and everybody knew it. If you'd had time to look at some of the photos in the office you would have seen Hamish in most of the pictures with a thin young woman, a good few years younger than yourself. Hamish never married or had any children. No one would have him really, so everything he had, emotionally and financially, went Toby's way.'

'Uh-huh,' I said. I wasn't sure where this story was leading, although it seemed to make more sense than anything Brian had said up until that point, so I let him carry on.

'Clifford had worked in insurance ever since he'd left university. He was the head of a big company, much bigger than Rogers, Parks and Justin, that employed over seven hundred workers. When he suddenly died from cancer, Toby was devastated. She could have kept the stocks and shares she inherited and let his money grow. The business was doing better than it ever had, but she wanted it put towards a cause that her father had *really* believed in.

'Her mother had passed away while Toby was still a teenager. Alzheimer's had affected her for over a decade when she eventually died. It was a terrific strain on the family. Clifford was very much in favour of the idea that she could be taken care of humanely, with a simple injection, or pills or some other chemical method. He campaigned for years to win the right to end her life, and of course, it was always denied. After Toby's father joined her mother in death, there was no one except Hamish to tell the poor girl any different. While she might have listened to him at one time, she wouldn't then.

'And so, I suppose, in his mind there was nothing left to do. Go along with whatever Toby said or did, regardless of the results – after all, she was the only person in the world that even seemed to *like* Hamish, let alone care for the old fool. I was there when she told him she was going to form a company that would carry out assisted suicides at a price.

'It was the company her father had always dreamed of. I saw the look in both their eyes, almost like . . . like two people that were so much in love. Each was unable to tell the other that what they were about to do was pure madness. And it wasn't an idle boast either. She'd had it all researched: plans, charts, a whole method of carrying out these suicides, so she couldn't be caught and he wouldn't be blamed. That phone number was just the tip of the iceberg.'

'So how *does* it work?'

Brian seemed uncomfortable, looking around the small café as though searching for enemy ears.

'I don't know much . . .' he cautioned, eyes not meeting mine. I waved him on until he continued. 'The phone number's registered under Hamish's name so Toby can't be found out that way. Until they catch her he can just pretend that he doesn't know anything about it, which is what he told the police the one time they did bother to show up. Toby's side of things is a little more complicated. I don't know the ins and outs, but the way she told it to Hamish, they set the company up in a cheap, almost disused building for up to four weeks at a time. They get clients in and take their money, then promise them suicide within a two-week period.

'When the month is up, they move out of the building. They take every piece of furniture and evidence with them, dust the place down for fingerprints, and Hoover bits of skin and hair for the DNA tests. I mean, these guys have got friends in the legal system all over the country, as well as doctors and scientists that work for them, so they know exactly how it's done.

'By the time anyone comes looking, Toby and her team are long gone. They disconnect the phone, perform the suicides and reappear in another location a few weeks later, ready to start again. New building, new receptionists, probably a whole new team – she was talking about everyone being on monthly rotation that day, God knows whether they went through with that. And that's it. Even if the police suspect anything, or have an angry family member swearing their loved one was murdered, there's never enough evidence to make a case, let alone bring it to trial. And that's how she gets away with it.'

'Jesus . . .' The set-up was a great deal more sinister than I'd expected. A handful of people killed every other month was a lot worse than anything myself, or Moore and Lindsey had anticipated. With so many victims, I couldn't understand why the detectives had to fight so hard to get a real investigation under way. The only conclusion I could come to was that no one knew how bad it really was. I lowered my voice, picking up on Brian's unease. 'How long has she been running this . . . business?'

'Around four to six years,' Brian replied. I whistled long and low. 'She brought the plans to Hamish around 1998/99, so I'm making a guess you know.'

'That's a lot of dead people.'

'Tell me about it.'

We talked some more about the company

86

and where Brian thought they might have moved to after Farringdon, though it was obvious each location was based on pure guesswork. After a while it seemed as though his earlier confidence had disappeared.

He still smoked, yet his hand trembled a little more with each puff. He wouldn't look at me straight. Maybe thoughts of the family he loved so much had finally hit home. Maybe he was thinking about that receptionist with his hand on the phone, watching us with unfriendly eyes. By that time, I certainly was. It felt like I was torturing Brian by making him stay seated another minute. I told him to go home, collect his family and book a hotel for a few nights until this all blew over.

'It's an awful risk you're taking,' I couldn't help but admit, once we'd paid up, grabbed our coats and were standing outside on the pavement. 'What's your problem with Hamish? Surely you were mates once. He must have done something pretty bad for you to confess all this.'

Brian grinned, tapping his nose and giving a violent shake of the head.

'It's all to do with money, Ervine. Those

stocks and shares. Hamish has been ripping Peter Justin and myself off for a very long time. He thinks we don't know what he's been up to, though he'll soon learn differently.'

He seemed to have got back his confidence at some point during this explanation. His head lifted and his shoulders fell back so that his broad chest poked out like a fighting cock. I was still worried about him though, so without thinking about it I gave him DS Lindsey and Moore's mobile and landline numbers. I told him to give them a call as soon as he got to a safe hotel and to tell them everything he knew about Hamish Park's dirty business dealings. After that, there was nothing more I could do for him. I left Brian on the same pavement I'd found him, hurriedly smoking yet another cigarette, watching me drive away. My lack of the power to protect him made me feel awful. Odd as he was, I'd grown to like the man.

Driving through north London, I couldn't stop thinking about Brian Rogers. I imagined his kids and Jamaican wife playing together in a large back garden, hugging and kissing like their lives depended on it. I pictured them as happy, sitting on deck chairs while a flaming red sun went down, high above them. He had taken a very brave risk in talking to me so openly. Thinking about his courage convinced me to try the phone number on the sky-blue card again. I pressed redial on my mobile. After a few seconds, there was a crackle and a phone began to ring, loud in my ear. I frowned and looked closer at the glowing screen. Had I dialled the wrong number?

'Good afternoon, Suicide Note?'

Shit. I hadn't expected them to answer. The voice on the other end was male, so he obviously wasn't my East-Asian friend, though it could have been the guy she was with when I was caught snooping around their office. Maybe Brian was right and the staff worked in shifts.

'Uh . . . hello, I was calling to make an appointment please?'

'There are no appointments necessary for advice against suicide. Would you like to come in right away?'

Against suicide? That didn't sound right. I wasn't letting them get away now though, regardless of my confusion.

'Sure. Can you tell me where you're based?'

It was an office block not far from Wood Lane, a long industrial road that ran between Shepherd's Bush and Harlesden. From the way the male voice described it, Suicide Note seemed to be on the Harlesden end. I wrote the details in my notepad, gave my name as Vincent Walsh and promised to be there within forty-five minutes. When I'd rung off and began the drive again, I tried calming my nerves by turning up the radio and thinking more pleasant thoughts about Brian and his West Indian family.

Unfortunately, that didn't work.

SEVEN

The Suicide Note reception area smelled of fresh wood and new paint. I sat across from the receptionist, trying not to look suspicious and not to fidget. Sweat was pouring from both of my underarms, trailing down my body all the way to my hips. It felt horrible, cold and damp, but I couldn't stop it. I was so nervous I was sure the man could smell my fear from where he was sitting.

With each passing moment I was convinced someone I'd met before would enter the office and recognise me. The consequences of being caught could be very bad. Despite what I was thinking, the receptionist totally ignored my presence. He was reading *Hello!* magazine and turning the pages with an almost angry intent. I watched him carefully and drank ice-cold water from a plastic cup, wishing I'd brought something to read for myself. I usually had a good book in my glove compartment for moments like these. All I'd brought with me today was my gun and the sky-blue business card. On the way to the office, I had an idea as to how I could use this interview effectively while keeping out of any trouble. Now I could only pray for the correct results.

The man pressed a finger to his earpiece, nodded as though he was pleased with himself and turned to face me. I could feel every muscle and tendon in my body.

'You can go through now, Mr Walsh.'

'Thank you.'

I walked towards a glossy black door in front of me, the only other door in the room besides the exit, trying not to seem overly self-conscious or self-confident. It was a difficult balance to maintain. I turned the door knob and without looking backwards, entered the next room.

It was quite a lot darker than the reception area. I stood by the door, my eyes adjusting to the light. When my vision righted itself, I could see shelves filled with books, a broad desk and an empty black leather chair before it, not unlike the one in my own office. My feet scraped against concrete as I walked towards the chair. There was a huge rug in the area around and beneath the office desk. Other than that, the floor was completely bare. The smell of dry dust rose into my nostrils.

I could make out the figure of a woman seated behind the desk, thin and young as Brian had described her. She was staring at me with eyes the colour of the sky above clouds – a thin blue that was almost white. She smiled, which made her angular face seem less severe as I stepped towards the chair. She didn't say anything until I was settled in, looking at me with calm expectation. I waited for her to speak, wanting to hear the voice that had sealed the fates of so many by their own approval.

'Mr Walsh?'

'Yes.'

'Mr Vincent Walsh?'

'That's right.'

'Welcome to Suicide Note.'

'Thank you.'

It was a perfectly normal voice. Pleasant, each word fully pronounced, spoken exactly the way the English language was meant to be. The woman before me was handsome in a stiff, unattractive way. Her hair was blonde and tied

93

back in a feeble ponytail, although it was easy to see that it was dyed, even in the thin light. She wore an all-black dress that would have looked the business on someone with even the slightest figure. On her it fell against non-existent breasts and shoulders that looked weak and tiny.

'My name is Toby Grantham. I'm the Managing Director of this company. How can I help?'

I'd already worked on my back story on the way over there, so it was easy to tell the tale of a man so beaten down by war and a lack of opportunity when he got home from all the fighting, that he immediately turned to drugs. After years of heroin and crack abuse he'd got into some bad drug deals with thugs from around his way.

This had resulted in his mother being threatened at knife point and ended in her untimely death from a heart attack. It had been back to the drugs for a long time after that, wallowing in self-pity and guilt until he'd seen the sky-blue business card on the floor of a tube train, late one Sunday night.

He'd picked it up and kept it for a long time.

Many months passed. When he eventually decided to kick the drugs and after the withdrawal symptoms died down, the nightmares involving his mother began. It had been two months since she'd been coming to visit him in his dreams, every night without fail. The man decided that he couldn't take any more of the visions and dialled the number on the card.

'You look in good shape for a recovering addict,' Toby said.

'I'm not like the rest of them. The army gave me discipline. No matter how bad things get, it's hard to let that go. A man's gotta have some kind of dignity in his life, don't you think?'

She smiled at that.

'That's what we sell here, Mr Walsh. Simple dignity, nothing more nothing less. Would you like a hot or cold drink?'

'Uhh . . .' What would my newly formed character say, I wondered, unsure what would look more suspicious, acceptance or refusal. I decided at once. 'Yes please. A cup of tea would be lovely.'

'Milk and sugar?'

'Yes please. Two sugars if you could.'

'No problem.'

She pushed a button on the desk intercom and asked the receptionist for one tea, one black coffee. I was hardly listening, wondering how I could get Toby to take the business card from me and then take it back without looking suspicious. If I could do that I would have her fingerprints, as well as Hamish's from earlier in the day. I would be nice, leave without signing any contracts and hand both cards to the police so that they could do their work.

There was a small box of cards on the table in front of me, exactly the same as the one in my pocket. Only these were violet-coloured instead of blue. Toby sat back in her chair and beamed. I pointed at the box of cards.

'Could I have one of those please? I lost mine.'

Toby blinked twice.

'Why ever would you need it?'

There was no threat in her voice, only simple logic. It was a good question and one I hadn't thought of an answer for.

'My friend was interested in what you do . . . He's been on the brown . . . Heroin, I mean . . . For near enough fifteen years. I told him I was coming here and he wanted to come too, but I didn't think it was a good idea.'

'You told him you were coming here.'

Toby made the statement in a flat voice. It was impossible for me to guess how she felt about what I'd told her.

'Yes. Is that okay?' I squinted over the desk. She seemed very distant all of a sudden, like a star in an otherwise empty night sky.

'It's fine, Mr Walsh. Although I think you did the right thing coming alone. We never interview two people at once.'

'That's what I thought.'

She passed me a violet card from the pile on the desk. I took it, put it in my inside pocket and sat back in the leather seat. Part of me was glad I'd got that over with. The other, more wary part warned me not to get too cocky. Toby's receptionist came in with our drinks, put them before us, nodded and left. A strong smell of coffee filled the room. Toby grabbed her mug and lifted it to her lips. She seemed in no hurry to speak, or even to get the interview under way. Most of the time she just crinkled her eyes and watched me. Sweat began to run from my armpits again.

'I suppose I should tell you what Suicide Note is about.'

I took a sip of my tea and let my head nod. The mug was very hot. I took a few large sips in a pale imitation of Brian Rogers. I started to feel even hotter, so I decided to wait a while before I drank again. I put the mug down. Toby was talking and I hadn't even been listening. That wouldn't do. I had to look normal, didn't I?

'. . . was formed by my father in 1980 . . . He thought that the laws on suicide were quite old-fashioned in some cases, including many that resemble yours. He founded this company to provide the service of assisted suicide in a human way, and to allow decent people the dignity of choice. First we'll take your details, then you'll be seen by an in-house psychiatrist who will check your mental status. A doctor will do the same for your physical well-being.'

'Why's that?' I asked, and almost jolted in my seat when I heard how deep and mumbled my voice had become. I could feel more sweat forming on my forehead and temples. It was cold, but did nothing to cool me down.

'They're checking to see if you're of sound body and mind, Mr Walsh. So that no one can say that you're unable to make your own decisions. When you've been passed and, providing you're still sure of things, you sign a contract with us. This bonds you to Suicide . . .'

I knew that she had stopped talking, although I found that I couldn't do anything about that fact because, all of a sudden, the movement of my body was not my own. Everything I did took way more time than normal. When I swallowed there was a bitter taste in my mouth, like cough medicine gone wrong. My slowed-down mind looked at the mug of tea, then up at where Toby Grantham was sitting. She was gone. I tried to glance around the room but the attempt at sudden movement made me feel dizzy and for a moment I couldn't see a thing. When my eyes readjusted there was Toby standing right in front of me.

'What . . . did . . .'

'Do you really think we'd let you come in here and pretend to be one of us without knowing where you'd come from? That you could barge in on a man like Hamish Parks and he wouldn't let me know? '

I stood up. Bad idea. My legs felt like those of

a newborn baby. I grabbed at everything I could to keep my balance, even Toby, who backed away and pulled the leather chair along with her. Left without anything to lean on, I took two small steps before collapsing on to the bare concrete floor. The thud shook right through me, making my teeth clatter. I rolled over on to my back. Toby was standing right over me.

'We provide a service, Mr James. That's all. A service for people who have nothing else. I'll be damned if some amateur detective who has nothing better to do than play like a real policeman is going to take that away from the people that need it. I swear on my father's grave, I'll never let that happen.'

She knew. I couldn't do anything about it though, trapped as I was by the paralysing effects of the drug they'd put into my tea. It must have been quite a strong dose because the world began to darken before I knew it and Toby's voice became a distant buzz in my ear rather than any real words.

The last thing I saw was a flashback from an earlier memory: the receptionist at Rogers, Parks and Justin staring at Brian and myself with a hand on his phone, a look of hatred in his eyes. After that there was nothing more than the blackness of my inner mind and the loneliness of sleep.

When I opened my eyes again, the darkness didn't go away. I gasped and tried to take in a deep breath only to find that it was impossible. My mouth was gagged. A loud noise that sounded a little like someone hurt and in great pain was close in my ears. I tried to move closer to the voice so that I could help the person, or at least intervene. It took a good few seconds more for me to realise that the tortured voice was mine.

Even then, when I recognised where the voice was coming from, I couldn't stop myself from attempting to yell. It was as though my body had a mind outside of mine with a life of its own, and that mind was looking out for me the only way I knew how. My first proper thought was that I was freaking myself out with that mournful sound. I had to stop myself, although I didn't know what I could do. I tried to relax, lie on my back and calm down. It was very uncomfortable. I managed it, even though something felt wrong, felt different about the position I had chosen.

After I'd managed to get my brain used to the fact that something wasn't right, I turned my attentions to how I was feeling. My head hurt. My throat did too, and my eyes felt puffed up as though I'd been out for a while. My ankles and wrists also felt sore, which probably meant that I was tied up with rope or some other strong material.

I couldn't tell whether the dark was due to a lack of light or some kind of blindfold that had been placed over my eyes. I had aches, bruises and itches that I couldn't get to. As soon as I noticed them they began to throb all at once as if competing for my attention.

Wherever I was, I had to get out of there. But I had no way of knowing if there were traps inside the room, or even if I was in a room at all. I lay back again, forcing myself to be calm. I took a number of deep breaths until my mind stopped racing.

When I felt less afraid, I let the breath flow out of me and then inhaled through my nose. There was, just beneath the smell of my own sweat, a hint of fresh wood and paint. Which either meant that I'd been left in the same room I'd collapsed in or I'd been moved to another in the same office space. My nose told me that it wasn't any further than that. I could relax a little. I probably wasn't in any major danger. Though I still needed to get out of this mess.

I tried to roll over and stand up, finding it impossible. For some reason I couldn't straighten my legs. I moved my hands up and down. The rope tugged at my feet each time I did it. I assumed that my wrists and my ankles had been tied together, which meant that I wasn't going anywhere in a hurry. I swore underneath my breath.

The fact that I could roll on to my back without pain meant that my gun had been taken from me, so even if I wasn't out of danger I had no means of protecting myself. I was lucky not to be dead already, I knew that to be true. This could mean that whatever I thought of Suicide Note's ethics, they believed murder in its conventional form was beneath them. It could also mean that they were biding their time in order to find a cleaner way to get rid of me.

A shuffling, scraping sound came from

somewhere. I was blind as a mole so I couldn't place where it was coming from. The sound grew louder and more urgent, until it turned from a quiet whisper into loud banging, which ended with a crash and silence that made me panic even more. I rolled around on the floor, trying to kick yet unable to do it. I wanted to scream but was unable to voice my anger. I waited for the needle to slip into my arm or the fatal blow to fall.

A hand touched mine and I went crazy, ignoring my bumps and bruises and rolling away as fast as I could, over and over again. People were shouting. I couldn't hear a word over my own muffled screams of terror. I felt more hands fall on my shoulders, arms and legs. They were trying to hold me still. Unfamiliar voices said my name over and over. I wouldn't listen and continued to scream.

Then I heard a voice I recognised instantly. It was female and at that point, probably the best sound I'd heard in my life.

'Vinnie . . . Vinnie, it's me, Carmen. You're okay. I'm here with the police, all right? You're safe now. Let me take the blindfold off, that's all we're trying to do. Can I take it off?'

I nodded madly. All at once there was light and I could see Carmen's face close to mine. I caught sight of many uniformed and plain-clothes police officers, Lindsey and Moore among them, before my eyes couldn't take the light any more and I was forced to shut them again. After that, all I could feel was Carmen's wet kisses on my cheek and her tears running down my temple as she hugged me.

EPILOGUE

My experience of being drugged and left for dead had been so frightening, it took a while for me to find out exactly what had happened. Carmen finally told me the full story when I'd been checked out of hospital with the all clear. I was lazing at home while Akira played in the back garden with Tanya, Dougie and my mother. It was two days after they'd found me bound and gagged in darkness.

I was lying on my sofa dressed in an old T-shirt and shorts with a blanket up to my chin. Carmen was sitting opposite me drinking a glass of fruit juice. She wore a short denim skirt and white tennis shoes along with a T-shirt that said, 'Trigger Happy, But We Ain't Laughing'. The T-shirt tickled me every time I read it, although it was hard to focus on the words. Every now and then Carmen would notice me trying and give me a stare that made me feel like a two-year-old. The doctors had warned I'd be woozy until the drug I'd swallowed left my body. It could take a week or so. Carmen had been almost military-like in her attention to my recovery and to be honest, it was beginning to get on my nerves.

'So, how'd you find me, Cee?' I asked for about the one-hundredth time since it had happened.

'I followed you up there innit?' she replied as though I was a moron. 'You'd been actin' all weird ever since dem detectives come to yuh office, an' I thought it wasn't like you to hide t'ings from me. So I borrowed Sadie's car and I was following you since the very first day. If I lost you I figured that Sadie would tell me where you were heading, but it only happened once, with Teresa Burrows.'

'Did you see what went on up at Suicide Note?' I said, sitting up in my seat while arranging my blanket so that I was still covered.

'Yeah, I saw everything, Vinnie. You went up there and disappeared for a while, like an hour. Then people starting coming out the building with boxes, files and stuff. That's when I got really suspicious, so I went round the back of the building and there were more people there, moving furniture, computers, tables and chairs – you know, clearing the place out?

'When I went back round the front I see that Grantham bitch walking down the street towards me like she didn't have a care in the world. She even nodded at me, Vinnie, nodded and said hello like she was the kindest person in the world. That's one evil bitch right there. She deserves to rot in a mental ward for what she done to you an' all those people.'

I agreed with Carmen, although I couldn't say a word. Knowing Toby Grantham's capabilities and the number of people her company had murdered, I counted myself lucky to be alive. I pretty much knew the rest of the story after that. As soon as she'd seen Toby leaving and the vans with office equipment drive away in a mini-convoy, Carmen had called Lindsey and Moore. They arrived not long afterwards with back-up, and rushed the empty offices to find me tied up in the middle of the floor, curled like a jellybean.

Between Carmen and my descriptions of Toby Grantham, they had enough to put out a warrant for her immediate arrest. If luck was with us, it would only be a matter of time before she was caught and brought to justice.

Hamish Parks had also decided to make a run for it. Police reports said that as soon as I'd left his office, he'd driven as fast as was lawfully possible towards a private airstrip owned by a friend just outside Oxfordshire. The police had caught and arrested him on the A40 past Slough, where CCTV cameras had spotted him. Realising how much of a wanted man he was, Hamish gave up without a fight.

If he'd been smart, taken some back roads and changed his mind on the way he might have got away with it. But by then, Brian had already spoken to the police and let them know that Hamish had fled, as well as his possible destination. The gruff solicitor had in fact been running full speed into a trap.

As crazy as the man had seemed when I met him, Brian Rogers had come through. It made me smile to think of the strange man with the pink Ozwald Boateng shirt, relaxed with his loved ones again.

'And that's that!' Carmen smiled, raising her glass of fruit juice. I lifted my own up to join hers, a gesture of salute to mark the debt I owed my old friend. 'Another James and Sinclair case successfully solved!'

'Solved but not forgotten,' I reminded Carmen, as I clinked my glass against hers.

WORLD BOOK DAY
Quick Reads

Quick Reads are published alongside and in partnership with BBC RaW.

We would like to thank all our partners in the *Quick* Reads project for all their help and support:

Department for Education and Skills
Trades Union Congress
The Vital Link
The Reading Agency
National Literacy Trust

Quick Reads would also like to thank the Arts Council England and National Book Tokens for their sponsorship.

We would also like to thank the following companies for providing their services free of charge: SX Composing for typesetting all the titles; Icon Reproduction for text reproduction; Norske Skog, Stora Enso, PMS and Iggusend for paper/board supplies; Mackays of Chatham, Cox and Wyman, Bookmarque, White Quill Press, Concise, Norhaven and GGP for the printing.

www.worldbookday.com

Quick Reads

BOOKS IN THE *Quick* Reads SERIES

Look out for more titles in the *Quick* Reads series being published in 2007.

www.worldbookday.com

**Have you enjoyed reading this
Quick Reads book?**

Would you like to read more?

Or learn how to write fantastically?

If so, you might like to attend a course to
develop your skills.

Courses are **free** and available in your local area.

If you'd like to find out more,
phone **0800 100 900.**

You can also ask for a **free video or DVD** showing
other people who have been on our courses and
the changes they have made in their lives.

Don't get by – get on.

FIRST CHOICE BOOKS

If you enjoyed this book, you'll find more great reads on www.firstchoicebooks.org.uk. First Choice Books allows you to search by type of book, author and title. So, whether you're looking for romance, sport, humour – or whatever turns you on – you'll be able to find other books you'll enjoy.

You can also borrow books from your local library. If you tell them what you've enjoyed, they can recommend other good reads they think you will like.

First Choice is part of The Vital Link, promoting reading for pleasure. To find out more about The Vital Link visit www.vitallink.org.uk

RaW

BBC RaW is the BBC's biggest-ever campaign about reading and writing. Find out more online at bbc.co.uk/raw or telephone 08000 150 950.

NEW ISLAND

New Island publishers have produced four series of books in its Open Door series – brilliant short novels for adults from the cream of Irish writers. Visit www.newisland.ie and go to the Open Door section.

SANDSTONE PRESS

In the Sandstone Vista Series, Sandstone Press Ltd publish quality contemporary fiction and non-fiction books. The full list can be found at their website www.sandstonepress.com.

Quick Reads

The Poison in the Blood by Tom Holland

Abacus

What was it that killed the Prince of Troy?

Legend tells that Hercules destroyed Hydra, a many-headed monster. Before her life was over, he dipped his arrows in her venomous blood. But how did one of these poisoned darts bring death to Paris, Prince of Troy and lover of Helen whose face launched a thousand ships?

Quick Reads

Danny Wallace and the Centre of the Universe by Danny Wallace

Ebury

Danny Wallace wanted to write about the Centre of the Universe, but how was he to get there? And what would he say about it when he did?

Luckily, in a small street, in a small town in Idaho, a manhole cover had just been declared the Centre of the Universe by the mayor. The science backed his decision and the town rejoiced.

And the name of the town? Wallace. It was a cosmic coincidence Danny couldn't resist . . .

Quick Reads

The Grey Man by Andy McNab

Corgi

Kevin Dodds leads a dull, uneventful life. He has a steady job at the bank, a nice house and car. His wife goes to bingo on a Saturday night, but he usually stays in to save money.

But one Saturday Kevin decides he'd like a night out himself. And he's not talking about a pint and a packet of peanuts down at the local. He's going to attempt to pull off one of the biggest bank robberies in history.

The priceless 'Augusta' necklace is being held in the safe of the bank where Kevin works. Armed only with information gleaned from the web, a Margaret Thatcher mask and climbing equipment he doesn't really know how to use, Kevin is about to take a heart-thumping step into the unknown. For once, he's going to stop being the grey man . . .

Quick Reads

Desert Claw by Damien Lewis

Arrow

In present-day Iraq thieves roam the streets. People are being killed in broad daylight. Security is non-existent. And now, terrorists have seized a Van Gogh painting worth £25 million from one of Saddam's palaces. They are offering it to the highest bidder . . .

Mick Kilbride and his buddy 'East End' Eddie are ex-SAS soldiers. The British Government doesn't want to pay the ransom money to the terrorists. Instead, it hires Mick and his team of ex-Special Forces to get the painting back. Their mission takes them into a dark and violent world where all is not as it seems. And if Mick and Eddie are going to stay alive, they're going to have to stay one step ahead of the enemy . . . and their betrayers.

Cleanskin by Val McDermid

HarperCollins

When career criminal Jack Farlowe's body is found washed-up on a Suffolk shore, it looks to the police like a clear-cut case. Broken-hearted at his daughter's death, he has drowned himself – good riddance and one less crime to solve, according to CID.

There again, maybe not. For, one by one, Farlowe's enemies are being killed. And the horrific manner of their deaths makes drowning look like a day on the beach . . .

Quick Reads

The Name You Once Gave Me
by Mike Phillips

HarperCollins

Daniel's getting married next week. He's got his future all worked out. It's his past that's the problem.

Daniel never knew his father. All his mother would tell him was that his dad had been a Nigerian who had died before Daniel was born. He didn't even know what his dad looked like until an old neighbour showed him a picture.

But the man in the photo is still alive . . . and now Daniel will stop at nothing to find him.

Quick Reads

I Love Football by Hunter Davies

Headline

Hunter Davies *loves* football. This book blows the whistle on his fifty-year love affair with the beautiful game. Here he provides an honest and funny look at why so many of us lose our hearts to footy.

Hunter explains the sport's history, the highs and lows of supporting a team, how it felt being at the 1966 World Cup, and what it's like meeting football legends such as George Best and Gazza.

Quick Reads

Winner Takes All by John Francome

Headline

Racehorse trainer Ben Sayers has two top-class horses to enter in the Cheltenham Gold Cup. One is owned by Alan Marcus, a ruthless businessman. The other belongs to Alan's gorgeous ex-wife, Christina.

Ben knows that both horses have an equal chance of winning. Unfortunately, Alan Marcus doesn't like competition. Especially when the competition is Christina. In Alan's world nice guys finish last. The question is just how nasty he will get . . .